Bits and Pieces
of my Childhood

BY
BARBARA RUBIN-KATZ

GARNET STAR PUBLISHING
BOSTON - LONDON - SYDNEY

Bits and Pieces
of my Childhood

DEDICATED

to the memory of my
dear son Raphael.

*Sculpture evocative of Raphael
by Barbara Rubin-Katz*

Literature, painting and sculpture are due to
express all the spiritual concepts which are
embedded in the human psyche, and as long as
any phase hidden in the psyche has not been
expressed, there is an obligation for the work of
art to express it.
-- *Rav Abraham Isaac Kook, Olat Rayah II, p. 3*

As quoted in
The Essential Writings of Abraham Isaac Kook,
edited translated and introduced by
Ben Zion Bokser, NY, 1988

Contents

Acknowledgments

There are many friends and family members who expressed interest and support for this project. There are a few individuals that I would like to single out for special thanks. First is my husband, Bob Katz, without whom this book would never have become a reality. He encouraged me, devoted countless hours to helping prepare the manuscript, as well as selecting illustrations and researching historical data. I love him for this and much more. I thank my sister Brenda who collected and organized family photos spanning over a century, many of which made a significant contribution to the book. She and my brother Neal were a source of much family history. Neal in particular contributed a great deal of the historical information included in the appendix. Bob's son Jonathan did a careful and thorough edit of the manuscript in its first stages.

My dear friend Roberta Warshaw created the beautiful design for the cover. Our friend Gloria Pless, provided "new eyes" for a final review of the pre-publication edition. Our publisher, Joyce Graff provided her professional expertise and critical judgment, in unifying all the "bits and pieces" into a beautiful book.

Finally, I wish to offer my special thanks to my late, great aunt Adeline, for publishing her memoirs, which preserved much family history and lore.

Reflections, a Self-portrait
A relief by Barbara Rubin-Katz

Prelude

As the proud matriarch of a large and ever growing family, I have an intrinsic bond with, and love for, each member of my family. They are a wonderful gift and a central part of my life. For the past few years, I have been thinking about my early childhood experiences and the impact they have had on my life. It is said that knowledge of your family's roots can give a deeper understanding of one's present and future life. These roots are what hold families together in love and shared heritage.

I've chosen these "bits and pieces of my childhood" in particular because they seem to show a sharp contrast between ordinary settings, ordinary people, and the ordinary rhythm of my life as a child; as well as random events of happiness, poignancy, sadness, and tragedy. Many of these events and experiences are still sharply etched in my mind. It is my pleasure to share these early memories with you.

Barbara Rubin-Katz

2015

1

Woodside Terrace — Early Childhood

My mother Jane Freeman Kurnitsky and my father Samuel Kurnitsky (later changed to Kurn) were born and grew up in Springfield Massachusetts, where I was also born and grew up. My mother dreamed of becoming an actress so she attended Emerson College in Boston, graduating in 1928 .

My father went to the University of Pennsylvania and majored in English. He was on the gymnastics team, and was the captain of the team in 1928, the year he graduated. In those days it was very unusual to have one parent who was a college

JANE FREEMAN
Springfield, Mass.
Jane seems always to be departing for or arriving from a week-end, and such nice exciting week-ends as they always seem to be! the kind to be described by "marvelous!" and "perfectly gorgeous!" and "oh, my dear!" You know the kind, and if you don't get Jane to tell you. She's the best authority we know of on the subject

The Emersonian, 1928

Samuel Kurnitsky (Kurn) in his gymnastics team uniform, University of Pennsylvania yearbook 1928.

graduate, and very rare to have two.

After graduating from college, my mother went to New York City to find work as an actress. Unfortunately, while there she contracted pneumonia. My father went to New York to take care of her and bring her back to Springfield. A year later (1930) they were married, and I arrived the following year.

The family's first home was on Woodside Terrace. My earliest memories of my first neighborhood began around the time I was 5. Beside my parents and me, our family consisted of three other siblings: my brother Neal (3 years younger), my sister Brenda (6 years younger), and my baby brother Sidney (12 years younger). We lived on Woodside Terrace until I was 14.

Woodside Terrace was a fascinating, gently sloping street, which I loved to roam, It began with a group of beautiful homes, but then abruptly changed into a strange collection of mismatched structures at the other end.

I remember walking by the comelier end with its nicely painted houses with trellises and pretty flowers. Often I would bump into a young girl close to my age who was large and unattractive. On these chance encounters I would get this tirade from her. "How do you think you would feel being like me? You are petite and pretty." (I never thought of myself as pretty, but maybe I was.) "You are so lucky to be like you are. Just think about that!" So I thought about it, and found that this was a surprise to me, but maybe she had a point. I hope she grew up to be a happier person.

There was a pretty yellow brick house in the neighborhood that I really loved, and I believe a part of me wanted to live there. It was neat and trim, quite the opposite of my home. I often wondered what kind of family lived there, and imagined that they were happy. Perhaps I was jealous.

I would walk up the hill, passing a few other appealing houses, and then, abruptly, the street changed. Like an unexpected wave, there appeared a large, ugly yellow four-story apartment house, trimmed in a hideous shade of brown. It just seemed to be plunked there, as if from a different neighborhood. The structure was just so incongruous with the beginning of my street.

Nobody ever seemed to be going in or leaving the apartment house, except, as I remember, two bullies we most often saw during the winter months. I recall when Neal and I made snow huts or snowmen, which would take us hours, those tormentors would promptly knock them down and laugh. I always wanted to fight them though they were twice my size. Even at that tender age, Neal was always a source of reason and restraint, and held me back. Maybe he was right because they were awfully large and clearly stronger than I.

Our home was located on the other side of the apartment house. It was a large two-family, tired brown, rundown house that had a porch in the front. The house badly needed a paint job. It appeared as if it needed plenty of work to fix it up. And, in fact, it did. After all, it was built in 1899!

Next to our home was a similar two-family house that was painted bright white. I did not know who lived there, but one day I saw the daughter of the house modeling her wedding gown. She looked so beautiful. But then her father and brothers came out on the porch. They were big, beefy men who were only dressed in their underwear. They sat there watching her modeling her lovely gown. The whole scene was so incongruous that it shattered any romantic illusions I might have had about her wedding.

One of the most interesting parts of the neighborhood was this enormous dark mansion that was painted black with a large lawn adjacent to it. As it turned out, this house belonged to the Buxton family who were owners of the Lady Buxton Wallet Company, which was founded in the 1890's and is still in business today.

We were told that there was something wrong with the Buxtons' daughter. She never appeared anywhere outside the house, which lent an air of mystery to the whole place. Given my vivid imagination, I thought she was sick, insane, or simply mentally impaired.

One had to be very rich to build a house like that, and there always was an eerie quality enveloping the structure. Only my brother Neal dared to get close to it.

One day Neal picked Lady Buxton's prized tulips and presented them to my mother as a gift for Valentine's Day. Lady Buxton saw this and came storming out of the house yelling at my mother. She was a hefty woman with a loud voice and all of us were scared of her, except for my brother Neal, who apparently was not.

Neal began playing pranks on Lady Buxton as a sort of revenge tactic for her outburst. One day he found a fishnet and proceeded to go fishing in her pond. He caught a net full of her prized goldfish, and he brought them back to my mother so she could cook them. And, of course, this did not go over very well with Lady Buxton. Neal even whitewashed her front steps once. It is a miracle she never called the police.

Ours was indeed a weird street. As we walked to the end of it there was another yellow building that was large and dreadful. It had very small windows with bars on them. No one ever seemed to go in or out of that place too. Once, I did see a nurse go into the building, but only once. In retrospect, I think it might have been a mental hospital.

Living, as we did, on such a peculiar street, it is fortunate none of us wound up in that institution.

Across the street there was a large empty lot with many maple trees. We loved to play there. Way in the back of the lot was a rundown little house, which everyone agreed was haunted. It had withstood many harsh New England winters, and part of its side was caved in. We imagined that there were ghosts in there, so of course, no one dared go in. But one day, I finally decided to look inside. I was terrified as I looked around. The house was as broken down on the inside as it was on the outside. The first time I went in, I quickly came back out. Of course, I told all the children watching that I was a very brave girl, and I really think they admired me for my courage. And on future visits, I found old newspapers, party invitations, and notebooks. Somebody had to have lived there a long time ago and eventually abandoned it.

At the edge of the lot there was a barbed wire fence, roots of trees, and garbage. Often, I would climb through a hole in the fence. Though difficult, it provided a short cut to a small grocery store. This huge effort saved me five minutes, believe it or not. And, of course, I had to come back the long way while carrying our groceries.

For a while, nothing out of the ordinary happened in our neighborhood, but then, seemingly out of nowhere, a great rain storm approached. It was a torrential storm, and as the rain fell harder and harder, it began to sound like rocks were hitting our windows. The accompanying thunder and lightning seemed to enter our very house. Weather reports had given us no warning of the impending tempest. Yet, there we were right in the middle of the worst storm I had ever experienced. As it kept increasing in intensity, the winds started pushing ever harder against our frail house until we thought it might collapse. News reports started coming over the radio. The bridge over the Connecticut River had fallen and people had been killed. We were frantic as my father had not yet come home. We were afraid that he might be lost in the storm. You can imagine our relief when he finally walked through the dront door, soaking wet. It was reported that trees were falling and soon we lost electricity and our house went dark. We feared for our lives. The storm's fury had spent itself by the next morning. Thus, we survived the famous surprise hurricane of 1938.

Upon leaving the house the next day, I saw huge trees uprooted. The roots looked like giant knives, black and sharp, sticking out in all directions. It was scary to see them pointing at me. We walked down the hill to see the main street flooded and people traveling in rowboats. This was no small trauma for a seven year old, and I will never forget what I saw that day. When I looked across the street at the field—believe it or not, our haunted house was still standing. This was indeed a miracle!

*82 Woodside Terrace, Springfield, Massachusetts.
Photo taken in 2014 by Neal Kurn. The building
has clearly been modified and refurbished since it was
built in 1899.*

2
Our Life at Home

O ur home was the first floor of a two-family
house. There was a long dark hallway as you
entered. At the end of the hallway there was
a big kitchen and beyond that was the bathroom,
which seemed to be the central room in the house.
There were no latches on the two bathroom doors,
and this led to some embarrassing moments.

To the left of the kitchen was my parents'
bedroom, and proceeding through their room were
the children's bedrooms, one of which I shared
with my sister, Brenda. We had a living room off
the hallway that we found dark and gloomy, and
we spent very little time there. In fact, the whole
house seemed somewhat drab as I remember, and
it was simply furnished with older furniture.

The relatively shabby appearance of the
house, both inside and out, exemplified how difficult life was at the time. An added factor was that
we were probably renting the place.

Because of the great depression of the 1930's
and the second world war during the first half of
the 1940's, life was a hardship for most people,
including us. There was very little money anywhere
and jobs were few and far between. My father, a
graduate of the University of Pennsylvania, had to

work in my grandmother's jewelry store. This was hardly what he must have dreamed of doing, and he probably felt disappointed.

My mother attended Emerson College in Boston, and as I stated earlier, went to New York with a dream of becoming an actress once she graduated. While there she contracted pneumonia, which in those days before antibiotics were used, was a very severe and life threatening illness. My father went to take care of her and had to bring her back to Springfield.

They were married in 1930, and I was born the following year. With marriage and a child, her dreams of becoming a great actress were unfortunately cut short. She did manage to have a brief career as a radio actress on WBZ-Springfield, and in small local theaters. So I had two parents whose

Old-fashioned General Electric washing machine. The woman in the picture is feeding a piece of clothing into the wringer, two rollers that pressed the water out of the clothes before they were hung on the line to dry. Picture source: History of washing machines on Pinterest.com

Bits and Pieces

life plans had been stymied.

The atmosphere in the house was some-what subdued and strained. No one was allowed to complain, get angry, or be upset. Somehow, we all understood this instinctively. Contributing to the atmosphere in the house was the fact that my mother was obviously unhappy, remote, and unaffectionate. She spent a lot time away from the house, so being the oldest child of the family, I felt it was my responsibility to fill in for her. As was not unusual for that time, I became "a little mother" at a young age. In this role, I often helped my mother do the household chores such as wash-ing the clothes, caring for my younger siblings, and even some cooking.

Washing the clothes and diapers was quite a production. We had an old washing machine with no spin cycle. This meant that the clothes came out of it dripping wet. They had to be put through a double roller to squeeze out the water by hand. There were no dryers in those days, so clothes had to be hung on a clothes line in the back yard using clothespins to keep them from blowing away. In the wintertime when we took the clothes off the line they were usually frozen solid. We would bring these frozen, rock-like objects into the house to thaw out. Often, we would drape them on chairs around the house. Sadly, after the whole process our clothes didn't look much cleaner than before. This was an arduous chore, and no matter how much I tried to help my mother, I watched her occasionally cry as we worked.

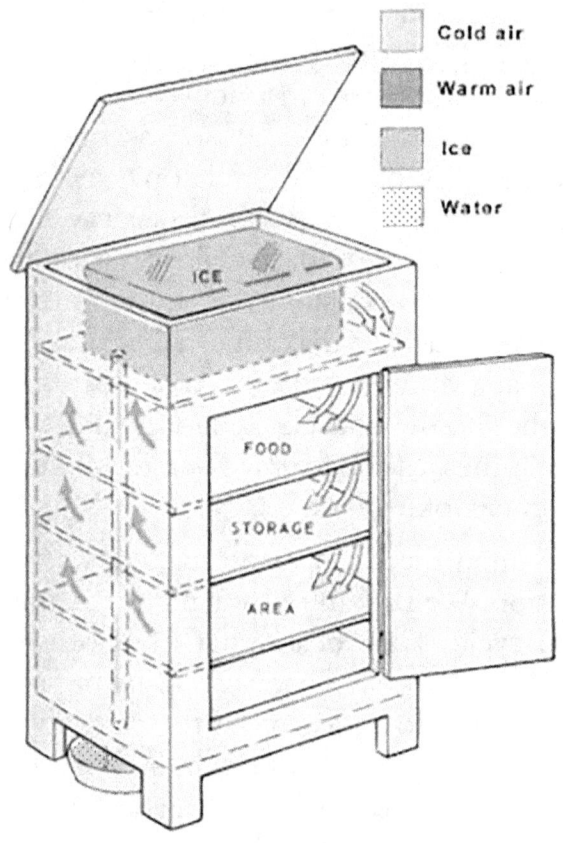

Cold air

Warm air

Ice

Water

This illustration shows how an "ice box" works.
The ice is placed in a large compartment at the top.
Since cold air sinks down, the cold air cools all the
shelves below. The warm air in the ice box rises,
accelerating the melting of the ice. The water from
the melting ice is directed to a tube which conducts the
water to a pan under the ice box.

Guess what, at that time we had no refrigerator! In those days many people didn't, so we used "ice boxes." Food was kept cool by a large block of ice in a chest with several shelves. The ice would slowly melt into a collection tray that had to be frequently emptied. Since the ice had to be replaced often, there was an "ice man" who delivered it to our home and placed it into the ice box. He would carry a large block of ice with an equally large pair of tongs. These blocks were about 18 to 24 inches on a side, so the "ice men" had to be strong. As you can imagine, we did not have any frozen food!

Another thing that was delivered to the house was milk. Every few days the "milkman" would deliver crates of milk in quart sized glass bottles and leave them near the front door. At the same time, he would collect the empty bottles, which were then washed for reuse at the dairy. The milk was not homogenized so the cream would rise to the top. Sometimes we would skim the cream from several bottles and make whipped cream.

Milk was delivered in a carrier like this, filled with fresh milk. The milkman would pick up the empty bottles we left outside the front door, and return them to the dairy for cleaning and reuse.

But, often I would wind up drinking milk heavily loaded with cream. As a child I hated the taste of that milk and I haven't drunk it since!

With respect to child care, I have two distinct memories. One of these was when I was very young. Neal was in his carriage on the front porch. I remember looking in on him and he didn't seem to be breathing. I quickly got my mother, who then ran out and looked at him. She grabbed him by his feet and kept slapping him on the back until he started to cry, which restored his breathing to normal. How she knew to do that I will never know!

Another thing I remember very clearly was when I was twelve years old and my brother Sid was born. He was an adorable baby and I love him dearly to this day. However, taking care of a baby was a struggle for me. One day he was very hungry and was crying as I was trying to prepare a bottle for him. It was necessary to pull a rubber nipple over a small opening at the top of a glass bottle which I was having trouble doing. I started to cry in frustration and called my father at work to ask him to come home and help me. He was very annoyed with the situation and made it clear to me that I shouldn't have bothered him, and that I should have been able to handle it on my own. With that he left the house telling me to feed the baby. It is hard to believe that this crying little baby would become a gifted doctor and musician.

I was also responsible for taking my brother to and from school. We went to the Sumner Avenue

School, which still functions today. In those days, children had to walk home for lunch. For us that meant a total of over a mile every day, rain or snow. In the spring and fall this was relatively easy, even with walking up and down the hills. In the cold Western Massachusetts winter, however, the trek became a chore. We had to wear our heavy clothes, consisting of woolen jackets and leggings, none of which were lined to cut out the wind. We also wore heavy rubbers over our shoes. Often, we would put on and take off these winter clothes four times a day. Walking is supposedly good for your health. If that is the case, we were probably the healthiest children in Massachusetts. At that time, there were no urban school buses and our mother could not drive. We had to contend with the elements constantly.

To add to our woes, we would occasionally be thrown into the bushes by a gang of bullies and be called dirty Jews. I also recall a girl sitting next to me in class saying "your God killed my

The Summer Avenue School as it looks today.
Photo by Neal Kurn, 2014.

The German passenger airship, Hindenburg, *caught fire and was destroyed in 1937 while docking in Lakehurst, New Jersey.*

God." Children can be taught hatred at a young age. There were no anti-bullying campaigns, nor was political correctness even a thought. So, we learned some hard life lessons early.

Although there were hardships, we experienced some very exciting moments as well. One day when I was six, I was on the playground at school with my classmates. We all looked up to see what seemed like the biggest hotdog imaginable. We observed that this giant hot dog had boxes under it where people were sitting. As it flew slowly over us, I almost felt that I could reach up and touch the vessel. It was such a wonderful sight. Of course, at the time we did not know what this strange thing was. Later we learned that it was a zeppelin called the Hindenburg, a lighter-than-air airship. Basically, it was a big balloon filled with hydrogen so it could float through the air. In the late 1930's it was a very luxurious way of flying from Europe to America. Most likely, the same day that I saw it, is when it historically crashed in

Lakehurst, New Jersey, while attempting to land. Because it was filled with hydrogen, an explosive gas, it blew up, killing nearly everyone on board. If you look up the Hindenburg on the internet, you can view old newsreels of the event. I am probably one of the few people who actually saw the Hindenburg fly!

One might question how children growing up when I did had fun and amusement without television, computers, smart phones, or video games. We actually did – and here's some of the ways. I was a voracious reader and used to haunt the little library that was about four blocks from our house. I came home with stacks of books filled with wonderful stories about interesting people and places. I was fascinated by these books.

Radio was also very important to us and we would hear delightful stories and dramas featuring the finest actors in the country. There were

Radios used to be big wooden pieces of furniture. This is a smaller table-top radio., the 1939 Sears-Roebuck "World's Fair" model made by Zenith.

My mother and siblings and myself in front of
82 Woodside Terrace.

scary shows like "The Shadow" and the "Creaking Door." There were quiz shows and there were comedians that were very funny. One of the comedy shows had Edgar Bergen and Charlie McCarthy. Edgar was a ventriloquist and Charlie was his dummy. When you stop to think about it, it is really ridiculous to be listening to a ventriloquist on the radio. How could you know that he was not moving his lips?

If you can believe it, there were sidewalks on all the streets, and these became instant play grounds for us kids. It was a place for games such as Simon Says and Hop Scotch. And, of course we would roller skate, bicycle, and jump rope.

Sledding was a favorite pastime of mine. I loved to sled down the steep hill behind our house. I would sled down and repeatedly trudge up again for hours. One time I hit a rather large tree hard and ended up with a huge bump on my head the size of a large egg. It didn't deter me. As you can guess, I was a feisty little girl. We also built snowmen, snow huts, and snow forts. There was a lot of snow in Springfield.

Saturday afternoons we went to the movies. In those days, if you were under twelve it cost ten cents for a double feature. If you were over twelve it was a whopping twenty-five cents. Somehow we managed to remain under twelve for an unusually long time. It was amazing, for that dime we got to see two movies, news reels, coming attractions, cartoons, and a serial. The serial was a short segment of an exciting adventure story, which made you want to come back week after week to find out how the hero or heroine escaped from the dire circumstances in which they were left. We were, as they say, hooked!

During Christmas each season I worked in my grandmother Kate's jewelry store. I sold all kinds of things, wrapped them, rang them up on the cash register, and said goodbye to happy customers. Not bad for a twelve year old! My grandmother Kate was a remarkable person and a shrewd business woman. It was her business that survived the depression and kept our family financially afloat. She was the most loving and attentive person in my life and took great interest in everything that I did. Neal and I used to spend a lot of time at her house, as it was just around the corner from ours. The high point of our week was going there and having Sunday lunch around a very large round wooden table. It gave me a very warm, contented feeling. During these visits, my grandfather Harry would sit in a large stuffed chair sucking on a stale cigar. He rarely talked to anyone as that would require taking the cigar out of his mouth.

A very special memory was when I was eight years old and my father took me to the 1939 World's Fair in Flushing Meadows, New York. A World's Fair is where many nations come to one place and build beautiful buildings to display their most modern architecture, art, and inventions, in order to give people a glimpse of what the future might hold. For example, at the 1939 World's Fair they were showcasing television. My memory was of many beautiful buildings designed in all sorts of shapes, and the brilliant lights that were everywhere. There were so many buildings and exhibits that it would have taken weeks to see everything. Now in retrospect, I hope that in one of those buildings there was a washing machine with a spin cycle.

3
Health Crises Hit Home

My parents had unusual attitudes towards illness. My father always denied that anything could be wrong with any of us; therefore, we were discouraged from complaining when we were sick. We rarely went to a doctor. On the other hand, my mother was so fearful of becoming sick that she would withdraw when there was any illness to be dealt with. So it was ironic that they were soon to be faced with two serious medical crises.

Unfortunately, my little sister, Brenda, had to go through a major ordeal at the age of three. She was an adorable child with blond hair and big eyes. When she began to learn to walk, she would drag her right leg.

One day my mother was in the park with Brenda. Unbeknownst to my mother, Brenda was being observed by a medical student. As he watched Brenda walk, he concluded that there was an abnormality with her hip. He approached my mother to tell her that he thought Brenda was lacking a hip socket and should have surgery. My mother explained to him that our doctor had said that "she would outgrow it." The medical student suggested that they take Brenda to Shriner's Hospital in Springfield for evaluation. Subsequently, she was evaluated there and it turned out that the medical student was correct in his diagnosis. The doctors at the hospital recommended surgery to rebuild her hip. Accordingly, a big operation followed.

After the surgery she was placed in a large body cast, which caused her to cry continually. My mother and I were standing outside the door to her hospital room, and I recall that my mother seemed to go into a strange state. Her face became twisted, tears rolled down her cheeks, and she seemed rooted to where she was standing. Although I was only nine years old, I begged my mother to go to Brenda, but she kept repeating that the nurse said that it would be better for Brenda to "cry it out." Apparently, at the time I disagreed, but I was ignored. Attitudes towards family involvement in the care of hospitalized children have changed dramatically and for the better over the last seventy years.

The memory of the agony caused by my mother's immobilizing conflict between her desire to comfort Brenda and follow the nurses directive has been painfully etched in my memory to this day.

Eventually Brenda came home, still in her large body cast with a worn-out look in her eyes. I tried to help care for her as best I could, but she was very heavy to lift in the cast. I felt so sorry for her. I loved her very much and it was sad to see her this way. When the cast was finally removed it was like a miracle had happened. She walked normally for the first time in her young life. I was so joyful to take her out and show the neighbors how beautifully she walked.

The other event occurred when my brother Neal was seven years old. He became very ill and we had to move him to my parents' bed. There was an eerie silence in the house, punctuated by Neal's rambling incoherent speech. My cute little red-headed brother was delirious. I realized how sick he was because a new doctor came to the house twice a day to check on him. It was shocking to have a doctor come to the house; especially given my parents' attitude towards illness and medical professionals.

Neal was so ill that he was eventually taken to the hospital. The diagnosis was spinal meningitis, a dangerous disease even now, but particularly then, prior to the use of antibiotics. Our house was quarantined and we were not allowed to leave for almost two weeks. Luckily, no one else in our family contracted the disease. I worried continually about my brother, especially after hearing my mother cry during the nights. At that point I realized that Neal might die and that I may never see him again.

In the hospital, he had nurses around the clock and I kept hearing that he had to be treated with sulfa drugs. Once again it seemed as if a miracle occurred. Neal beat the odds and had a full recovery. Sadly, one of his nurses contracted his highly contagious disease and died.

The hospital bill for two weeks came to $72! Neal has the bill to this day as a keepsake.

Upon his return home we got a call from the hospital, and they explained to us that he had been exposed to measles, also a serious disease at that time as there were no vaccinations for the disease.

Subsequently, Brenda and I contracted measles. We both had large raised red spots that itched and hurt. We were not allowed to scratch them. I felt wretched and Brenda seemed immobilized. We were very sick.

At some point during our illness, our mother had to go out. Neal chose this opportunity to jump out of a window and run down the street. I dragged myself out of bed to go to the window and shout for him to come back, which eventually he did. When we were all fully recovered I was so happy to be able to walk back and forth to school with him again.

4
The War Years

One Sunday, I walked into our living room, which was unusually dark, even for that room, as no lights were turned on. I found my father and grandfather, Harry, sitting as if their ears were glued to our big old radio. They were listening intently with nervous looks on their faces. Since my grandfather rarely came to our house, this was an unusual sight.

I could hear the voices of commentators describing how airplanes had flown over Pearl Harbor and bombed our naval fleet. Several large battleships were sunk, and thousands of sailors had been killed or wounded. To add to this frightening news, the planes that were bombing the ships were Japanese.

I was ten years old at the time and was very curious about what was happening. It seemed very difficult for my father to explain it all to me. The date was December 7, 1941, and as President Roosevelt said in a famous speech, it was "a date that would live in infamy." This was the start of our country's entrance into World War II.

I had never heard of Pearl Harbor and was amazed to learn that there was a part of the United States in the middle of the Pacific Ocean.

Everyone was shocked that so many planes had come all the way from Japan, which seemed so far away, and that the attack was a total surprise to our military. We lost a lot of our Pacific Fleet that day, and America started the war at a great disadvantage.

Many people were worried that the Japanese would invade the west coast. The bad news just kept coming in non-stop. My grandfather and father appeared to be shocked and worried as well. This frightened me more than the news itself. Of course, the entire event was incomprehensible to me at my age, but it caused tremendous anxiety.

Uncle Aaron home on leave, with Barbara and Neal.

Although we were mostly sheltered from the war for the first few years, the effects would become more tragic as it went on. When the war began, we were ordered to draw dark shades over all of the windows of our house so that no light would escape at night. My father was an air raid warden. His job was to walk around the neighborhood and make sure everyone's shades were drawn and the blackout was complete. He had to wear a steel helmet and carry a powerful flashlight. We were told that yet another enemy, the Germans, who had declared war on us a few days after Pearl Harbor, might bomb the east coast. Thus, the government ordered blackouts on both coasts. We were also told that submarines and aircraft carriers could reach America.

Uncle Sidney home on leave with his wife Millie.

Springfield, where we lived, was a major manufacturing center of rifles for the army, and therefore, was considered a prime target for any German air raid. In spite of these obvious signs of the war in my own home and community, as a child, I had little comprehension of the gravity of the situation or the toll the war was taking on our country.

Within our family there was little discussion about the progress of the war and its consequences, even though Brenda used to listen to the war news regularly on the radio. For example, I was aware that food and other things were rationed. I did know that many people had victory gardens to supplement the families' food supplies. But I was only vaguely aware of all of the death and destruction in Europe and the Pacific.

One thing I remember clearly was seeing gold and silver stars in neighbors' windows. A gold star meant that the family had a member killed in the war. A silver star was for a wounded soldier.

The effect of the war would soon hit us in a personal and serious way. Many young men throughout the country, sons and husbands, volunteered or were drafted to serve in the armed forces. There was hardly a family that did not have someone who was serving in the armed forces. As for our family, my father was the oldest of four brothers. After my father there were Aaron, Maury, and Sydney, the youngest. One day we learned that my father had received notice to report for a physical exam to determine if he was fit for military service, and perhaps to be drafted. As children, we reacted with some amusement and disbelief because he had a consistent cough and did not seem healthy enough for the military. Furthermore, he was in his late thirties, and to us that seemed too old to become a soldier. Yet, we were also apprehensive that they might take him anyway. The day of his exam he was gone for a long time, and when he returned home he had a rather sheepish look on his face. He explained to us that he had flunked the exam, and that they told him that he was physically unfit for duty. Additionally, having four children rendered him exempt from the draft. I remember feeling so relieved when I heard the news.

My Uncle Aaron went into the Army and served in the Pacific Theater for most of the war. He never talked about what he experienced, but I do know that he spent some time in Australia. One time, I saw a picture of him sitting next to a large tent looking very serious.

It is told that before the war Aaron was a real playboy. However, after he returned from the war, he was subdued and quiet. He also became very religious and remained so for the rest of his life.

Maury did not get drafted into the service. He seemed healthy, but he had several children, which may have put him low on the list.

My father's youngest brother Sidney joined the Aviation Branch of the Navy in his mid-twenties and became a pilot. He was a handsome young man, who was loving and affectionate. He paid a lot of attention to me, always teasing me and making funny jokes at my expense. He had the air of a movie star, with his red hair and smile, and I adored him. I remember on one of his visits home he was wearing his white uniform and seemed very proud of himself. Little did I know that this would be the last time I would ever see him.

One Sunday the whole family was gathered at our house when the phone rang. Aunt Edith, my father's only sister answered the phone and her face turned ashen. I remember her first words were, "are they looking for Sidney, and did they think they could find him?" She was speaking to my Aunt Millie; without anything further being said, we knew that Sidney's plane had crashed. He had been on training maneuvers over the Chesapeake Bay when his plane crashed, killing him. The silence in the room was so profound it was as if everyone stopped breathing. We were all in shock and sat immobilized. It was incomprehensible that this wonderful man was dead and I would never see him again, and it took us all a long time to accept the reality of this.

When Millie, his wife, came back to Springfield, she was pregnant and in deep mourning. She cried constantly and probably never completely recovered from the tragedy. She had Sidney's daughter, Sunny, in 1944. Several years later she remarried. Sadly, when Sunny was five, Millie died of leukemia. Sunny was raised by her maternal grandmother. So the reality of the war struck the family in a tragic way, and it forever shattered my childish innocence.

On a more pleasant note, I remember one day in 1944 during President Roosevelt's last election campaign, Brenda, Neal, and I went to the train station with my father and uncle. The President was making a "whistle stop" tour around the country, as part of his election campaign. In those days before television was widely used, presidential candidates would charter a train, stop at every town on the route, and make speeches from the back of the train. These were called whistle stop tours. Large crowds of people would come to the train station to see and hear them. Seeing the President of the United States was a great thrill for all of us.

5

Summers
in the Berkshires

When you leave the Springfield area heading west on the Massachusetts Turnpike, very soon you will see in the distance low lying, beautiful mountain tops. In certain light, they have a mystical quality. When you leave the turnpike, you soon are driving along lovely country roads, passing by lakes, forested areas, farm houses, and pastures. Interspersed are quaint rural villages with modest houses and large estates. This is the heart of the Berkshire mountains, which has been a wondrous place to live since the early 1700's, and a vacation destination since the 1880's. Its beauty has made it an inspiring place for many artists, writers, and musicians.

Since the mid 1930's, the Berkshires has been the summer home of the Boston Symphony Orchestra at Tanglewood. With its vast rolling lawns and beautiful vistas, there is no wonder why so many come to enjoy the concerts.

One of the estates in the area was the home of Daniel Chester French, a famous sculptor. It is a gracious, large estate. Located at the side of the main house is his studio that still houses many of his original tools and small works.

There is a sculpted seated figure in the studio. It is told that this sculpture, after its creation, was shipped to New York City for a time where two expert stone carvers replicated the small piece into a monumental sculpture. The enlarged version was shipped to Washington, D.C., and it was installed on the Mall in 1922. To this day, the dramatic seated figure of Abraham Lincoln is viewed by millions every year.

For several summers in my youth, my family and I loaded up our car in Springfield and headed off on the old back roads to the Berkshires. At that time the turnpike didn't exist, and the older roads made it seem as if we had driven hundreds of miles (in reality it is only about 45 miles from Springfield).

We did not travel to a proverbial Berkshire mansion for vacation, but rather to a large farm in Otis called Rod's farm – a working farm owned by a family of Jewish farmers since 1904. On the premises there was a large farmhouse where some of the rooms were turned into guest rooms. To the left of the farm house there was a large dining and recreation shed, and to the right of the house was a huge barn filled with cows and heaps of hay. I fondly remember milking a cow. I really loved that barn.

Across the road from the farmhouse there were eight to ten rustic bungalows, one of which was our summer home.

Most of the guests at the farm were families from New York. Usually, the fathers were there only on weekends. They would leave early Monday morning to return to work in the city. Fridays were always a big event because a bus would pull up around five in the evening. From it, a group of tired men in rumpled suits would exit to be greeted by their wives who stayed on the farm during the week.

As you can see, we were left in a very unusual world consisting only of women and children for most of the week. In our present era, when most women work, I doubt such a lifestyle still exists.

Because we were living in this community of mostly married women, we were intrigued by the lives of the few single women visiting the farm. One story involved a young woman called Louise − a friend of my mother's − and her growing romance with one of the Rods' two sons. I would see them walking together holding hands and swimming in the lake. They seemed so happy together. Soon I heard that they wanted to get married.

The older brother, however, was very angry about this. He stormed into our bungalow one day, and he said that his brother and Louise were both crazy and that they were too young to get married. I guess that since Louise was a friend of my mother, he thought she could influence her. My mother did not get involved, but the older brother continued to try to break up the romance, and sadly, he was successful.

Later on Louise married a very unattractive, miserable looking man, and was very unhappy with him. She had long talks with my mother crying that she wanted to leave him. At this point, my mother took a stand and persuaded Louise to stay with her husband. Louise decided my mother was right and stayed with him. I always envisioned her being unhappy her whole life, and was sad for her. It was hard for me to understand how adults could be so senseless of their own needs.

In spite of all this drama, it was a free and easy time for us children and I really loved that farm. There were a lot of things that we enjoyed doing, especially blueberry picking. Almost daily, Neal, Brenda, and I would venture into the blueberry patches. Each time we went, we traveled further and further from the main road and discovered wonderful new groves of blueberry bushes. One day we were out for an unusually long time, and eventually walked back home proudly carrying two big buckets of berries. We must have been out too long, because my mother and several of the other women were waiting for us with worried looks on their faces, and they seemed relieved to see us. They probably thought we were lost or kidnapped.

One scary day for me was when I went running through a field. A massive dog ran out barking viciously, caught up to me, and then started to scratch my back. I ran sobbing and screaming to the barn. After someone pulled the dog away, the farmhands made a big circle around me and taunted me for being frightened. Actually, I think the farmhands terrified me more than the dog. Obviously, these farmhands were not very good child psychologists, and to this day I'm uncomfortable around dogs.

One day while we were near the barn, my mother noticed smoke coming from our bungalow. She ran towards it faster than I had ever seen her move. Once inside the bungalow she found Neal in bed pretending to be asleep while the window shade was on fire. Neal had an enormous capacity to get into trouble. As cute as he was with his red hair and winning smile, he really got a spanking for that prank! Another incident that added to the drama of our stay at Rod's farm had to do with a deep pool in an old quarry near the farm. Neal was sitting on a very large boulder overlooking the pool. He either slipped or jumped into the pool. This was a serious situation since he did not how to swim. He floundered around some, but luckily some unknown man dived into the pool and pulled him out. Given all of Neal's youthful escapades, it is remarkable that he grew up to be champion of the law and a community leader.

Our summer at Rod's farm ended with a frightening event. One night we looked out of the window and saw the barn ablaze with flames that looked like they were reaching the sky. I went into shock, and for hours I couldn't move away from the window, I was transfixed. The fire engines arrived and the firemen worked for a long time to no avail. The barn burnt to the ground. It was a terrible loss for me as I had so many fond memories of that barn, and for many nights I could not sleep. This was a gloomy way to end our stay at Rod's farm.

From what I know, the Rod family continued to operate the farm until 1970's. Today, when you drive by where the farm was, you will see only one small house on the property. I believe that descendants of the Rods' still live there.

After our few years summering at Rod's farm, we did not move on to fancy hotels or bungalow colonies. Instead, we merely drove down a steep hill from the Rods' and came to our new summer home at Pyenson's Chicken Farm. This farm had been owned and operated by the same large Jewish family from about 1906 until the present.

The patriarch of the family came from Russia, where he was trained as an agriculturist. After immigrating, he and his wife worked in New York City for a few years, but he missed living in the country. He eventually found a job on a farm in the Berkshires. Several years later, a nearby farm in Otis went on the market. Luckily for him, the Jewish Agricultural Society loaned him eight hundred dollars to buy the farm. I believe the year was 1906. By the time we began to summer there, it had become solely a chicken farm.

The main structure at Pyenson's was a quaint farm house. We stayed next door in a two level bungalow on a slope. It had an outdoor wooden stairway that led down the slope, from the bed rooms and family room upstairs to the rustic kitchen and all-purpose room downstairs. The way the bungalow was situated, it looked as if it could tumble down the hill at any moment.

At the bottom of the hill there was a wooded path, and at the end was a lovely lake where we went swimming, row boating (when there was someone strong enough to row the boat), and fishing. We experienced many happy times at that lake.

At night we occasionally built a bonfire, toasted marshmallows, and sang songs. We simply enjoyed being by the water because it was so attractive and peaceful.

I used to love to dance barefoot on the grass in front of the bungalow. Sometimes, boys driving by would give an appreciative whistle. Between the bungalow and the lake there was a gentle knoll that created a private, secluded space where my mother and some of her girlfriends would sunbathe topless. They were way ahead of the Europeans! To my knowledge they were only seen once by a young boy from the farm. This of course, led to all sorts of excitement.

Across the street from the farm house was a huge barn, and more importantly, next to it was a large field filled with dozens of chicken coops with chickens clucking day and night. It took some time to get used to this, but after a while the sound became part of the ambiance of the farm.

One of the most interesting summers at Pyenson's farm was in 1943, and the memories of that summer are fondly etched in my mind. There was a large extended family visiting the farm house, and a constant flow of friends and relatives visiting our place. Since we really only had two bedrooms, it's hard to conceive how we managed to accommodate so many people.

It was a sheltered, insular life that protected us from the reality of World War II. Although we had a large old radio, it mostly provided music with only some occasional news.

The experiences at the farm during this summer represented a microcosm of the human condition, both happy and sad. There was the expectation of new life, as four pregnant women were all due to have babies that fall. They were

Some of the women at Pyenson's farm, 1943.

my mother, who was pregnant with my brother Sidney, as well as two of my aunts, and the farmer's wife, Audrey.

My Aunt Jerry was married to my Uncle Aaron who was serving with the Army in the South Pacific. My Aunt Millie had been married to my Uncle Sidney. Since he had just recently died she was in a constant state of grief. It was tragic to watch.

Audrey, who was from New York, had been a swimming counselor at a camp near the farm when she met and married Max, who was the Patriarch's oldest son. I would sit with her for hours while she made clothes for her family-to-be. She went on to have five children who grew and multiplied, and have now produced the fifth generation of Pyenson's on their farm. She was a loving hard working woman who died at the age of ninety-three. She was active in the local Jewish community until the end. I remained in touch with Audrey until shortly before her death.

Sadly, some of my mother's other friends who came to visit had hard life experiences. For example, there was Mary Golden, a pretty little librarian from Boston, who was sweet but unhappy. Her story was indeed something to be sad about. She lived for many years with a married man in her mother's Boston home. As I recall, he had promised her that when he got divorced he would marry her. However, when he finally did divorce, he ended up marrying someone else. Understandably, this was a major shock for Mary. Later on she developed all kinds of ailments and died a few years later at a rather young age. I suspect she really died of a broken heart.

One of our visitors was Dora. She worked in my grandmother Kate's jewelry store stringing pearls. She was a quiet, sad woman who had no children. She always took an interest in what I was doing. One Saturday afternoon when she visited us on the farm, she went with my mother to the Jacob's Pillow Dance Theater, the mecca for modern dance in America. When they left I was home alone, and shortly thereafter, I heard heavy footsteps on the stairs. Then the kitchen door slammed, and in stomped a huge man with a loud, menacing voice demanding to know where Dora was. I was a small twelve year old child, and quickly became frightened by his threatening demeanor. At first I hesitated to tell him where she was, but he became angrier and more intimidating. Finally I agreed to take him to Jacob's Pillow and reluctantly got into his car.

When we arrived at Jacob's Pillow, which was about four or five miles away, the performance had not yet started. At that time there were no chairs and the audience sat on the floor. Dora's husband walked toward where she was sitting near the stage. He grabbed her by the arm, roughly pulled her up, and said "come on Dora let's go!" And to my horror, he dragged her out of the theater. She turned bright red and as she passed by me, I saw she had tears in her eyes. I had never witnessed such abuse before, nor would I ever again. I felt guilty and cried, but I could never have imagined what he was going to do. Afterwards, I would see her when I went to work in the store and she seemed slightly embarrassed and sad. I can only imagine what she had to put up with in her life.

During that summer my father began to cough a great deal. The belief was that driving back and forth between Springfield and the mountains once a week may have caused the recurring cough. In retrospect, this seems a bit of a farfetched theory; however, the cough worsened over the years and led to his having severe respiratory issues. His condition would eventually change all of our lives.

Meanwhile, during that summer my father started to draw. He would find old barns and houses and sketch them. As other people had before him, he too was inspired by the beauty of the Berkshires. This new interest would lead to a lifetime of painting landscapes, still lives, and portraits. He had a remarkable talent.

The summer of 1943 was the most memorable of all my summers in the Berkshires. It will always have a special place in my heart.

44 Washington Road
Springfield, Massachusetts
Photo by Neal Kurn, 2014

6

A New Life on Washington Road

I n 1945, we moved to a lovely new home in a nicer Springfield neighborhood called Forest Park. Our street was named Washington Road, and all of the houses were well maintained and attractive. The house, even though it was old, seemed very elegant — a sharp contrast to our house on Woodside Terrace. I really loved living there.

It had a large front porch and a central hall with a stairway that went to the second floor. Upstairs, there were five bedrooms off of a hallway that was lined with floral wallpaper, which to my young eyes seemed quite beautiful. I even had my own bedroom. Downstairs, there was a large sunny living room, a dining room, and a spacious kitchen. I have little recollection of the kitchen, probably because I had to do so much cooking there. I never did enjoy cooking!

We lived two blocks away from Forest Park, a large and peaceful public space used by the community. It became the center of our world. My friends and I would meet and spend many happy hours there simply "hanging out." To this day I

My siblings and I, happily ensconced in our new home.

have not seen a park as lovely. It had several tennis courts, bike paths, baseball fields, a zoo, and a large lake that froze in the winter. I loved to ice skate on the lake; it felt like I was flying through the cold air with total freedom. Neal also started his lifelong passion for tennis on Forest Park courts.

Bicycling in the park was one of my passions and I was somewhat of a daredevil. Once, I went full speed down a steep hill, lost control of the bike and tumbled over and over, passing out next to a lily pond where I finally stopped. Neal, who was with me, thought I was dead. Someone called my father to come and get me. Although I was bruised from head to toe, my parents did not take me to a doctor, as was their custom. I guess they assumed that I hadn't broken any bones.

One jarring note in this idyllic setting was an incident involving a very young couple who were "going steady." I often saw them together in the park. The boy was the son of the principal of our junior high school. At some point, the girl apparently wanted to break up their relationship. Unfortunately, this must have enraged the boy because he ended up shooting her to death in the park.

Since the park was the center of all of our lives, this upset us greatly. In spite of this tragedy, however, life in the park eventually resumed its normal rhythm and we still enjoyed being there.

Living at home was easier at the new house for me compared to living in our old one. We had household help a couple of days a week, and my mother was around more, taking care of Sidney who was a one year old when we moved to Washington Road. My sister, Brenda, was six years younger than me and was a beautiful and sweet child. I used to enjoy walking through the park with her and going to the zoo. She liked to take ballet lessons at the time, and there is a striking

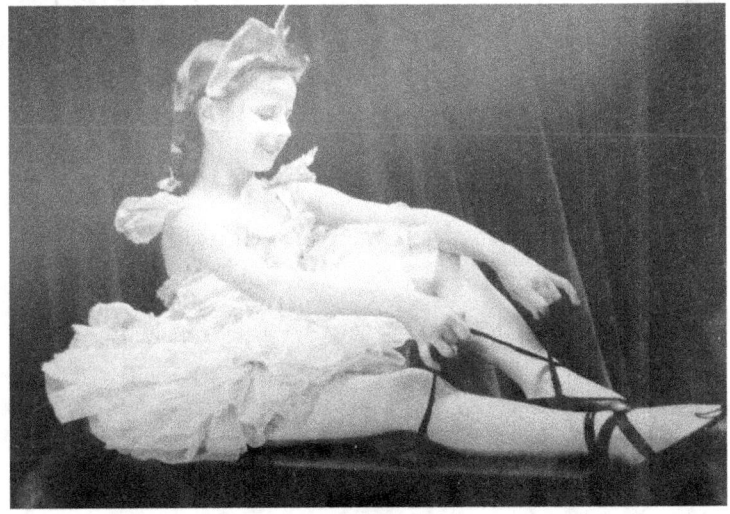

Brenda in her tutu

picture of her gracefully seated on a bench wearing her tutu.

My Uncle Maury and his family lived down the street. Brenda spent a lot of time playing there with her cousins, especially Inez, who was her best friend. Although we lived only three houses apart, Maury never visited our house. Similarly, my father never visited Maury's house. Years later I learned that Maury had been in love with my mother. When he was away at Harvard my father entered the scene and wound up marrying my mother. Obviously, bad feelings arose between the brothers.

Meanwhile, my father's respiratory issues became more severe. As a result, someone had to shovel coal into the furnace as he could not, and I was the lucky recipient of the job. Our coal was delivered in a truck that would connect a chute to our basement window. Coal would be dropped through the open window into our large, open coal bin. I had to open the door of the furnace which was near the coal bin, and was greeted by heat and flames. This really freaked me out. Then I had to go to the coal bin and shovel coal into the fiery furnace. After a few shovel loads, I felt like I was being roasted.

During this time, my social life was going well. I frequently went to the Jewish Community Center that was near our house. It was in an old mansion, and they had many programs including dances, which I loved. I also worked at the Center's summer camp as a counselor where I made many friends. Both my friends from camp and school enjoyed socializing and we had many parties.

It was ironic that my mother, who always wanted to be a dramatic actress, was constantly at the center of ongoing soap operas at our own home. One in particular revolved around her older brother Percy. Percy went to Harvard, but other than that brought little joy to the family. His first wife, Ruth, reportedly was beautiful, but unfortunately she died giving birth at Boston City Hospital. The baby survived and was named Ruth, but was always called Pixie. She was given to her maternal grandparents who lived in Gardner. They took care of her for three or four years after her mother's death. They were warm and loving people.

Percy remarried to a woman named Minty, who was an abrasive and unpleasant woman. One day the couple appeared abruptly in Gardner with the objective of taking Pixie from her grandparents in order to raise her themselves, and Pixie was taken to their home in Boston. I'm sure this caused the grandparents grief and sorrow.

After four or five years of marriage, Percy and Minty divorced. Minty decided she wanted to legally adopt Pixie. This was a very unusual legal case because she was not the child's natural mother. A bitter court case ensued, and the story ultimately appeared on the front pages of the Boston Globe. Things became so rancorous that the judge decided to send Pixie to live with us to remove her from the turmoil and to diffuse the situation. The opposite happened!

Pixie came to live with us, taken from the only mother she really knew, and was desperately unhappy. She would go to the attic and scream for hours. Then she would come down, have more temper tantrums, and say vile things about us that she probably heard from Minty. She would frequently kick us, particularly Neal. She also tried to run away on several occasions in the hopes of getting back to Boston. She had very little money so she never got very far, and my father would have to go pick her up and bring her back. Percy was rarely around, but when he did come over he was highly critical of me in particular. He would accuse me of not taking good care of Pixie and not preventing her from running away. This of course, made me angry at him and I always sulked in his presence. Even at the age of fourteen, I had realized it was not my responsibility to take care of his daughter, it was his. He taunted me because I never smiled in his presence, and at the time I did not realize how emotionally charged this situation must have been for Pixie.

Minty eventually won her custody battle and Pixie returned to Boston to live with her step mother. After this, we visited Minty and Pixie in Boston several times. During these visits I noticed that Minty had Pixie acting as a waitress in her home; having her serve the food and coldly ordering her around. Poor child! Eventually, Pixie married Minty's younger brother. Percy eventually married again, and his third wife was also an unpleasant woman. Apparently, when Percy died he left Pixie out of his will. Sadly, somewhere along the way we lost all contact with Pixie.

After Pixie left our house life returned to normal, and it became peaceful and pleasant at home once again. The war was over, and the family seemed to be doing better financially. Sidney was still a toddler. Neal, Brenda, and I were beginning to blossom, finding new interests and friends, and we were coming into our own. Life seemed easier and happier. However, my father's illness would eventually bring new challenges and changes to our lives. But this would come several years into the future.

Barbara dancing on the lawn.

7

Grace Notes

W hen I was twelve years old, I entered Forest Park Junior High School. It was a huge, dark, and bewildering place. We had to move from room to room in order to change classes — something totally new for me. The first day of classes I lost my school bag and it took me three days to find it. In today's schools, it probably would have been stolen!

Despite the gloominess of the surroundings, ironically, it was here that some of my artistic talents began to emerge. I had always loved to dance, and I remember my dance debut in seventh grade. We had class in the gym and the teacher was attempting to teach us a dance routine, having us stand in place and using our bodies in an artistic way. Suddenly, the teacher stopped the class and called out to the back of the room where I was practicing. "Young lady, would you please come to the front." Although she was pointing in my direction, it took me a while to realize that she was actually pointing at me. When I came to the front of the class, she said, "You do this so nicely, would you do it for the class." So I did the whole routine and every one applauded. It was a big moment in my young life.

Shortly after that experience I started taking ballet lessons, but I found them to be boring and constraining. They came to an abrupt end when the news of President Roosevelt's death was announced in class. My dance teacher lashed out, saying that she was glad that he was dead and that he had done a great disservice to the country. Since my parents had an unconditional adoration of him, I found her comments very upsetting and wouldn't continue my studies with her. So much for ballet! Later on, through high school and college, I learned to enjoy modern dance, which allowed me greater freedom of movement.

I also had a musical debut of sorts — banging away at the piano, keeping the rhythm going for the junior high orchestra. We were a small group of beginners, but we made up for our lack of virtuosity with our great enthusiasm. I learned to play the piano from my first teacher, my Aunt Edith, who lacked interest in teaching. She was a serious, rather humorless, unhappy person, as was her husband Joe, a lawyer. They never had children. Perhaps that was why she was so unhappy.

As a teacher, Edith was rather stern, business-like, and not too inspiring. She had a huge black grand piano that she never played. She also had cabinets full of sheet music of what seemed to be the entire classical piano repertoire. I was told that she had studied at the New England Conservatory of Music in Boston. Sometimes I would ask her why she never played her piano, and I was always greeted by a stony silence. So, Edith and her piano remain a mystery to me and continue to tweak my curiosity.

She didn't last long as my teacher. She passed me on to a musician friend named Ben. He lived in an old house where every room was painted in a warm yellow. I liked that color more than the piano lessons, even though Ben was a warm, happy man. Unfortunately, like Edith he did not have children and did not seem to enjoy teaching. I remember, at one point, he had me repeating a measure from a Beethoven sonata until I was close to tears. It is ironic that I played the piano on my own for most of my life and loved it despite the fact that Edith and Ben seemed to give up on me. I must have been a reasonably good pianist because I taught my children, and they've turned out to be very good musicians.

Interestingly, I later learned that Edith and Ben were romantically involved, but my grand-parents didn't think that a musician was a suitable match for their daughter. Edith's parents were wealthy at the time and thought a lawyer or doctor would be more suitable for their daughter, so they broke up the romance. In time, Edith married a fellow named Joe and had a sad, empty life. Would life have been happier for her if she had married Ben? Who can know?

Eventually, the family made the decision that I should quit the piano and study the cello. Ever compliant, I agreed. At first the cello seemed so big and cumbersome with four heavy strings and a bow. To produce the notes one had to press the strings down at various intervals with the left hand while at the same time draw the bow across the strings with the right to produce the sound. That took a good deal of coordination! It seemed a hopeless task in the beginning, but I eventually caught on. And so I started many years of enjoyable and fulfilling music making.

Within a relatively short time after starting high school I began to play well enough to form a trio with two of my musician friends, Ellen on the piano, and Mona on the violin. We called ourselves the Orpheus Trio. We became very popular and played at weddings and special events. We even were paid for these appearances. So I guess you could have called me a professional musician. Not bad for three high school kids!

When I was in the eleventh grade, I auditioned and was accepted into the Springfield Youth Orchestra. In some orchestras, people compete to become the leader of a section (i.e., first violinist, first cellist, and so on); however, I was given a place near the back of the cello section and was happy to be there. We rehearsed in a beautiful room at the Museum of Art where there were marble pillars and tapestries surrounding us. And, we gave our concerts in the huge Springfield Concert Hall — a very elaborate building.

During one rehearsal, the conductor announced that he wanted to see the whole cello section in a room off the main hall. He indicated that he had given a lot of thought to the sound of the cello section and he decided he had to make

Miss Mona Fieldman and Miss Barbara Kurn, Classical High School students were among the eight local musicians participating in the two hour program of the Massachusetts All-State High School Orchestra last Saturday afternoon in Boston's Symphony Hall. Miss Kurn, daughter of Mr. and Mrs. Samuel Kurn of Washington Road, is a cello pupil of Miss Flora Cross Kinsey. Although she has studied the cello for only two and one-half years, she was selected over all other Massachusetts high school students to occupy the first section of the cello section. Miss Fieldman, daughter of Mr. and Mrs. Harry Fieldman of Narragansett St., an honor student who is a pupil of Albert Raisis, played with the first violins. The young musicians are well-known locally for their performances with the Orpheus Trio which includes Miss Ellen Orlen, pianist. Harold C. Youngberg, director of music education in the public schools and Alexander Lesile, director of the Springfield Symphony Orchestra, selected the young players, whose performance proved very effective. -- *Springfield Daily News,* March 1948.

changes in the seating of the cellists. Then he looked at me and said, "Barbara I want to make you be first cellist." I was really surprised since I had not been playing a long time. The girl who had, up until then, been first cellist gave me looks that could kill. Music can be a pretty cut-throat activity! So, for two years I led the cello section in many concerts and thoroughly enjoyed my new role.

In my senior year, I was selected along with another cellist to represent Springfield in the Massachusetts All State High School Orchestra. We rehearsed and gave a grand concert in Boston's famous Symphony Hall. Playing in such a historical and musically rich building was an amazing experience.

Looking back, I believe my Aunt Edith and Ben did me a great favor by suggesting I leave the piano and study the cello. Actually, I've played both instruments most of my life and have always enjoyed them.

Barbara Kurn,
High School
graduation

8
Going West

Early in 1948, my father visited Tucson, Arizona, for about four months because he was told by his doctors that he needed a warmer, dryer climate. He had been suffering chronic respiratory problems for the previous five years and his breathing and coughing had become increasingly worse, and at times, he required long periods of bed rest. Back then we did not have the kind of medicines available today for such illnesses.

While he was in Tucson he sent us photographs of him looking fit and happy. He told us that he was doing a great deal of painting. Considering everything, mainly his health and well-being, a decision was made for the family to move to Arizona.

This decision would bring an enormous change in our lives. He bought a house in Tucson, sight unseen by my mother, and then returned to Springfield to organize our move. So began the huge task of selling our house, packing our belongings, and heading out west. For my parents, who had spent their whole lives in Springfield, this had to have been an emotional experience. However, for me and my siblings, this seemed to be a grand adventure.

On a warm sunny day in August of 1948, we loaded our car, a big old red Pontiac, with all manner of possessions. My mother hung several heavy wool winter coats inside the car in case it got cold. Little did she know what was in store for us once we reached the southwest.

There was a send-off party that included my Aunt Edith, several uncles and, surprisingly, my grandfather Harry who rarely visited our house. He complained bitterly about our leaving, did not seem to understand why we were going, and was angry about the whole thing. Everyone looked rather sad and worried, including my parents. They had spent their whole lives together in Springfield. In those days of limited travel, Arizona semed really remote for our relatives and friends. We might as well have been going to the moon.

We waved goodbye, climbed into our non-air conditioned car, and started the journey. Our father instructed us as follows: "When I turn right everyone should lean to the left, and when I turn left everyone should lean right." So much for his confidence in the stability of our packed car! In those days cars had no seat belts, no automatic transmissions, and tires of very questionable reliability. Hoping for the best, we finally headed off.

Of course we started going west by heading south. First, we headed to Baltimore, Maryland to visit Aunt Millie, my Uncle Sidney's widow who was hospitalized for leukemia. At the hospital our parents were allowed in her room, but we children were not. After a while my parents came out of the room and my mother had tears in her eyes. Sadly, Millie died shortly after this, leaving her five year old daughter, Sunny, motherless. Sunny came to live with Millie's mother, as mentioned previously.

From Baltimore we progressed into the Deep South, and Brenda clearly remembers seeing signs saying "toilets for whites only," "swimming pools for whites only," and "drinking fountains for whites only." We were driving through the South at the peak of the segregation era. Thankfully, in another twenty years segregation would be illegal.

As the days wore on my father, who wasn't well to start with, became very tired. Since my mother didn't know how to drive, and I had some Drivers Education training in high school, he asked me to drive even though I didn't have my license yet. We were going through rural areas where the towns were few and very far apart. Of course, I managed to take a wrong turn that took us two hundred miles out of our way before anyone even noticed!

Having a non-air conditioned car was a bit of a challenge given the fact that there were six of us crowded in a confined space, during the hot, humid southern summer days. Although they will deny it, either Neal or Sidney (I forget which) threw up a lot, so the car really smelled rank.

Because of the heat and humidity, along with the smell of vomit and our fatigue, it was a very tough, seemingly endless trip. For me, however, it still seemed a great adventure even though the destination was a mystery — sort of like a big surprise party. Somewhere along the way we got rid of the heavy, woolen winter coats.

After many days, we finally arrived in Arizona several hours east of Tucson. I remember that my mother went into a small roadside grocery store and bought a loaf of Wonder Bread and a package of sliced cheese. We made sandwiches, and because the air was so hot and dry, it was as if we were eating toasted cheese sandwiches without having to use a frying pan. Such was our introduction to the arid summers of Arizona. As we approached Tucson, we were all tired, hungry, and apprehensive.

When we finally drove up to our new home, we saw that it was small and neglected. I remember noticing that the lawn consisted of overgrown bushes, grass, and beer bottles. About a week's worth of advertising flyers were also strewn near the front door.

After a moment of silence in the car, my mother suddenly burst into tears. It would be a while before she looked happy again. We gathered our courage and our few belongings and walked into the house. As we entered the house, we found it similarly neglected and hot, just like the outside. There were two small bedrooms, one bathroom, a tiny living room, a dining area, and some sort of screened sleeping porch. How were all six of us going to live here, I thought? It was half of the size of the house we left behind in Springfield.

Our first priority was to cool off the house. It took some time, but my father finally figured out how to get the "swamp cooler" working. (A swamp cooler works by evaporating water from wet straw mats, which cools the air flowing past. They only work where the humidity is very, very low) It seemed to take forever to get the house cooler. Because the swamp cooler vents were located in the ceiling of the small hallway by the bathroom, my siblings and I proceeded to sit on the floor under cooler vents for long periods of time. Occasionally, we took turns going outside to face what we called "The Beast."

The sleeping porch became Neal and Sidney's bedroom, and Brenda and I shared the smaller bedroom. It was distressing to me that in

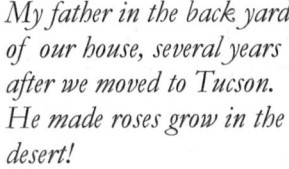

My father in the back yard of our house, several years after we moved to Tucson. He made roses grow in the desert!

Barbara in Arizona with a Saguaro cactus.

a period a few years we had moved from a shabby two-family house, to a lovely large home, and then to this tiny, neglected place.

Tucson, it turned out, was not like living on the moon as we had imagined. Most homes in our neighborhood were small, one floor structures made of stucco with flat roofs. In 1948, Tucson was considered a small city with about 50,000 people. It has since has grown to about a million as of this writing.

Our home was situated on a flat desert valley that had all kinds of cacti, especially the giant Saguaros, which can grow ten to twenty feet high and can hold 5000 to 6000 pounds of water (you don't want one of these cactuses falling on you). The only place in the world that these giant succulents grow is in the Sonoran Desert located both in Arizona and Mexico.

Tucson is ringed by several high, rugged mountain ranges, which are quite dramatic. The endless sky is turquoise blue from one horizon to the next, and the desert dust creates spectacular sunsets. The stars at night are bright and most constellations are visible even in town — an astronomer's dream. This magical desert was a playground where we would picnic, hike, and ride horses.

Truthfully, for some of us the first few years in Tucson were very difficult. Eventually, however, like the Saguaro, we were able to put down broad roots and make new and happy lives for ourselves.

CODA

W/hen I arrived in Tucson I was 17 years old. At that age you can't imagine where life will take you. As I think about my life now, many years later, it's like a long dream. The pathways of my life, as with all lives, have taken many different turns. My life since Arizona and onward through adulthood can best be described as, intense, complex, busy, yet greatly fulfilling, and full of love. I think of my life with awe and gratitude that so many good things as well as hard times happened. My life has been like listening to a beautiful piece of music, with high and low notes, dramatic interludes, and a myriad of themes. At some point the music stops, yet the melody still lingers in one's mind and remains in one's dreams. In part, I believe that the beauty of Arizona was an inspiration and a springboard to future accomplishments.

After four years at the University of Arizona studying to be a teacher, I changed my focus. When I graduated in 1952, I decided to start my adult life by moving back east. I went to Boston, enrolled in Simmons College, and received a Master's degree in social work. My professional focus for many years was in the human services. In 1955, while living in Boston I met and married Emanuel

Rubin, a medical student. After Emanuel (Manny) graduated from Harvard medical school, he went into the Navy, and we moved to Tacoma, Washington, where I had my first child, Raphael. Fifteen months later I gave birth to my second son, Jonathan Isaac, in Tucson. In 1960, my third son, Daniel, was born in New York, where Manny was doing a residency in pathology. In 1964, a much hoped for daughter, Rebecca, was born. Rebecca's birth also occurred in New York where we all lived for about ten years. In the early 1970's we moved to Great Neck, Long Island. We bought a gracious and old, vine covered, Normandy styled home. Our back yard soon became a sports field for every kid in the neighborhood. As a result, our neighbors put up a high fence. I was, and still am, inordinately proud of all my children. They grew and thrived and were a boisterous lot.

As always, music played a major role in my life and that of my family. While in college, I was a cellist in the Tucson Symphony Orchestra (the TSO was started in 1928, and is the oldest symphony in the southwest). When I lived in New York, I played in the Queens Symphony Orchestra and the Great Neck Symphony Orchestra. It was during one rehearsal of the GNSO that a young, very small cellist came to rehearse a concerto with us. Thus, I had the once in a lifetime experience of playing with Yo-Yo Ma who became the greatest cellist in the world.

Unfortunately, at age 40 I had neck surgery that caused nerve damage to my right arm and I was never able to use the bow again. However, I could still play the piano fairly well. I had always been highly involved with teaching music to my children. I taught all of them the piano, and then started two of them on the cello, and two on the violin. Despite their objections, I got them to practice a great deal. People would say to me, "how can you do this to your children?" However, much later in life, my kids would say, "why didn't you make us practice more?"

When my three sons were in high school, they all played in the Long Island Youth Orchestra. Once a year, the Orchestra traveled to distant countries such as Brazil, Australia, or New Zealand. Jonathan was given the opportunity to solo on Brazilian National Television and solo at the world renowned Sydney Opera House in Australia. The children continued to play concerts when they went on to college, followed by medical school for the boys, and law school for Rebecca. And, they still continue to play today.

While living in the New York area, raising my children and enjoying my musical activities, I managed to get a Master's degree in public health at Columbia University. I worked in both individual patient therapy and administration, and I published several professional papers on patient advocacy resulting from my work.

In 1978, Manny accepted a job in Philadelphia and the whole family moved there. I took a job at the Federation of Jewish Agencies as the Associate Director of Planning. During this period, our marriage became strained and we each took different paths. We were divorced by 1984. Later that year, I traveled to Israel to visit Daniel, who was serving in the Israeli Defense Forces. Although I had traveled to about twenty different countries, this trip turned out to be life changing. While in Israel, I met Bob Katz, a research scientist who was in charge of the Army's ceramic research laboratory near Boston. He was a keynote speaker at an international scientific meeting at the same hotel in Jerusalem where I was staying. It was Chanukah, a very festive and happy time. Bob and I became fast friends and soon fell in love. We were married a year and a half later. It was the second marriage for both of us, and I happily acquired two more children, Pamela and Jonathan.

Prior to meeting Bob, I had begun to explore new artistic outlets that would satisfy my creative needs. I began to study sculpting, and was fortunate to study with some famous sculptors in Philadelphia and Boston. I knew I would have problems with my vision due to a genetic disease called

Sketch of Robert Katz done by Sam Kurn, 1987

Bits and Pieces

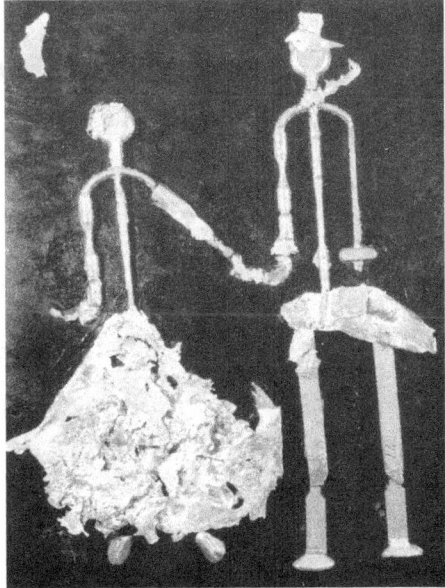
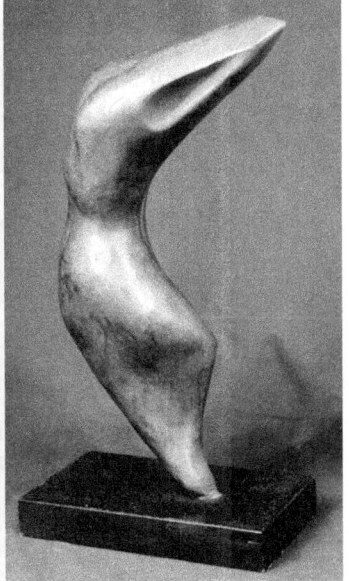

Sculpture by Barbara Rubin-Katz:
Left to right, top to bottom: Beckoning; Celebration II;
Stepping Out; Winged Torso

retinitis pigmentosa. I thought at the time that as my sight diminished, I would be able to work by touch. As it turned out, even as my eyesight worsened, I still used my remaining vision as difficult as that was. But after about twenty-five years I had to stop entirely, which was very traumatic for me. I did have a pretty good run as a sculptor and had the opportunity to exhibit my work in many galleries and art shows, and I received awards for my work. I am most proud of being named a Copley Artist by the Copley Society of Boston (America's oldest art association). This is a competitively earned distinction.

When Bob and I were married in 1986, we bought a lovely three bedroom condominium in Brookline, Massachusetts, where we still reside. It has large windows overlooking the Boston skyline and is convenient to all of the city's amenities.

After Bob retired, we bought a small townhouse in Tucson to escape the cold New England winters. In Tucson, we now get to look at a different but equally dramatic skyline, the beautiful mountains that encircle the city.

Over the years, five of our children married and have produced large families of their own. We now have 32 grandchildren and a growing generation of great-grandchildren, currently numbering thirteen. We have had many wonderful celebrations of weddings, bar and bat mitzvot, britot, baby namings, birthdays, holidays, and anniversaries.

Sadly, in 2011 our son Raphael passed away

after bravely struggling for three years with a brain tumor. He was an extraordinary son, father, husband, doctor, and musician. Each year he gave a solo violin concert before an ever increasing audience numbering in the hundreds. He was truly a Renaissance Man. He was much beloved by his wife Rene, his seven children, family, and his many friends, and we miss him very much.

In spite of life's tragedies, there is always a reason for hope. Two citrus trees grow in our patio in Tucson, one of which is a grapefruit tree. This tree is very old, and a few years ago it was dying. Everyone who looked at it, including a professional arborist, shook their heads and said "cut it down." However, Bob was undaunted; he worked on that tree consistently and conscientiously with love. He trimmed and pruned, fertilized and watered, and applied all conceivable tree medications. We left Tucson in early April. When we returned the next January – behold, what did we see? The tree was loaded with grapefruit.

This tree is a metaphor for life. With love and caring there is always the potential for renewal. I have been fortunate to have experienced many such opportunities for growth, change, and renewal in my life. For this, and my large and wonderful family, I consider myself truly blessed.

Appendix

A FAMILY TRADITION OF JEWISH COMMUNITY SERVICE

As I was thinking about my family, past and present, I realized that over six generations many individuals have made significant contributions to the Jewish community. They all devoted substantial amounts of time, effort and in many cases funding to their causes and institutions. It seemed important to share their names and chronicle some of their contributions with you.

GENERATION ONE

Abraham Barowsky (1858-1925) - my great-grandfather
- Officer of Congregation Rodphey Shalom, Holyoke, Massachusetts

Abraham arrived in the United States in 1893. He had just completed his service in the Czar's Army, as a clarinetist in a military band. He had a long red beard. This hair color trait has appeared in succeeding generations. He was known for his strict Orthodoxy. His daughter-in-law Adeline recounts a story to illustrate just how strict he was. One Sabbath in Rodphey Sholom, a certain man was reading from the Torah. Abraham objected to his being permitted to read on behalf of the congregation, as he felt the man was not a "shomer Shabbos" (a strict Sabbath observer).

So Abraham jumped on the bimah (platform), grabbed the Torah reader's ear, and dragged him to the front door of the synagogue. As Abraham was about to eject him, the poor man turned to him and is reported to have said, "OK, can I at least leave with my ear!"

GENERATION TWO

| *Ida & Isaac Kur-
nitsky ca 1900* | *Kate & Harry
Freeman ca 1900* | *Adeline & Jack
Barowsky ca 1916* |

Ida Barowsky Kurnitsky (1884-1932) - Abraham's daughter, my paternal grandmother

- Leader of The Daughter's of Zion Organization and a driving force in their creation of the Daughters of Zion Home for the Aged. Springfield, Massachusetts, ca 1905-1912

- President of Springfield Hadassah

Jacob "Jack" Barowsky (1892-1977) - Abraham's son, my great-uncle

- Chair of the Holyoke United Jewish Appeal

- Recipient of the Louis G Marshall Award of the Jewish Theological Seminary, New York, New York

- Recipient of an Award for Outstanding Service to Israel, presented on behalf of the State by Gen. Moshe Dayan, 1958

Adeline Seamon Barowsky (1885-1990)

Ida Barowsky Kurmitsky (standing far right) with the founding committee of the Daughters of Zion Home for the Aged, Springfield, Massachusetts, ca 1910.

Bits and Pieces

- Jacob's wife, my great-aunt

- Recipient of the Woman of Valor Award by the Women's Israel Bond program, presented by Drew Pearson, the famous radio commentator, 1966

Jack's company, Adell Chemical Company, invented the famous household detergent, Lestoil. Detergents were a new product and most consumers were used to soaps or scouring powders. So Jack was continuously trying to raise the public's awareness of the benefits of his product. In 1954, he hit on the concept of using short repetitive TV ads with catchy jingles. Jack the chemist not only invented Lestoil – he invented the advertising technique known as "saturation TV". It worked and Lestoil took off like crazy. And the catchy jingle "it takes less toil – when you use Lestoil", became a piece of 1950's Americana! By the way you can still buy it, and it's pretty good.

Adeline relates that her father and John Fitzgerald were friends (yes, John "Honey Fitz" Fitzgerald, Mayor of Boston and the grandfather of JFK). When Adeline was a very young girl, her father took her to one of the "Honey Fitz" campaign rallies. Fitzgerald spotted her, lifted her up on the stage and said, "Now this is the little girl who inspired my theme song. Let's all sing to her 'Sweet Adeline,'" which everyone in the hall did.

Adeline's parents both came from Neustadt, Lithuania. Bob's father's family also came from Neustadt and that is where his father grew up, before coming to America at the age of 14. At our wedding Adeline and Bob's Aunt Riva started exploring the Neustadt connection. Riva, learning that Adeline's maiden name was Seamon (and realizing that in Neustadt it would have been spelled Ziman), concluded that Bob's family and Adeline's family were next door neighbors in Neustadt. Is that *bashert* or what!

GENERATION THREE

Kate Freeman with baby Jane, about 1907

The Freeman family about 1920: left to right, Kate, Jane, Percy and Harry

The Kurnitsky family: left to right: Sam and Maurice in the back; Edith, Isaac, Ida and Aaron; Sidney on the floor in front, ca 1928

Edith Kurnitsky Swirsky (1904-2002) - my aunt
- President of Springfield Hadassah, 1940s

Samuel Kurn (1906-1992) - my father
- Executive Director of Temple Emanu-El, Tucson, Arizona, the oldest synagogue in the Territory/State of Arizona, 1949-1977.
- Principal of the Religious School

Jane Freeman Kurn (1907-1997) - my mother
- Hillel Director at the University of Arizona during the 1950's
- With my father, coached approximately 2000 B'nai Mitzvot at Temple Emanu-El, 1949-1987
- Wedding coordinator at Temple Emanu-El, ca 1950-1987

The religious school at Temple Emanu-El was renamed "The Jane and Samuel Kurn Religious School" shortly after their retirement.

Aaron Kurn (1909-1994) - my uncle
- President of Kadima Synagogue, 5 years in the 1960's, Springfield, Massachusetts

Maurice Kurn (1908-1965) - my uncle
- A founder and President of the Springfield, Massachusetts, Jewish Community Center

The Family name was changed from Kurnitsky to Kurn on 27 October 1942

Jane and Sam Kurn Religious School, Tucson, Temple Emanu-El, being visited by their grandchildren, Abby and Jonathan Rubin, 2013

GENERATION FOUR

Jane Freeman Kurnitsky with daughter Barbara, 1932

Barbara Rubin-Katz - the author, daughter of Jane and Sam Kurn
- Associate Director of Planning, Federation of Jewish Agencies, Philadelphia, 1978-1984

Robert Nathan Katz - Barbara's husband
- Board Member Temple Israel, Natick, Massachusetts, 1979-80
- Chairman of the Board of Temple Beth Zion Brookline, Massachusetts, 1999 to 2003

Neal Kurn - my brother

- Co-Founder of the Jewish Community Foundation of Greater Phoenix, 1971; subsequently chaired the Foundation
- National Chair of the Endowment Fund Committee of the Council of Jewish Federations, 1983-86
- President, Jewish Federation of Greater Phoenix 1987-89
- The Jewish Federation of Greater Phoenix Medal of Honor Award 1986

Barbara "Bobbi" Agron Kurn - Neal's first wife

- Chair of the Women's Division, Jewish Federation of Greater Phoenix 1985
- Chair of the Women's Division, United Jewish Appeal of Greater Phoenix
- The Jewish Federation of Greater Phoenix Medal of Honor Award 1989

Neal and Bobbi were the first couple to have ever received these awards based on each of their individual achievements and contributions.

Albert Sterman - my sister Brenda's husband

- Hebrew School teacher, Nogales, Arizona, 1961-1970

Sidney Kurn - my brother

- Pianist for the Chabad of Santa Rosa, California, Klezmer Band, 2014-present

GENERATION FIVE

Barbara and her daughter Rebecca

Raphael Rubin, my son, and his wife Rene Rothstein Rubin - They worked jointly to:

- Create and Fund the Kohelet Yeshiva Art Room, Lower Merion, Pennsylvania, 2009
- Create and Fund the Rubin Life Sciences Center at Kohelet Yeshiva, Lower Merion, Pennsylvania, 2011

Raphael Rubin, my son

- Member of the Board of Directors of the Jewish National Fund of Greater Philadelphia, 1995-2010

Rene Rothstein Rubin - my daughter-in-law

- Founder and Artistic Director of the Annual Dr. Raphael Rubin Memorial Concert at Kohelet Yeshiva, 2013-present

Jonathan Isaac Rubin - my son

- Founder and President of Agudath Israel of Florida, 1998-present

- Founder and Vice President of the Vaad HaKashrut of Miami-Dade County, Florida, 2004-present

- President of Yeshiva Toras Chaim-Toras Emes, No. Miami Beach, Florida, 2013-present.

- Past President of Congregation Ohr Chaim, Miami Beach, Florida, 1991-93.

Abby Boxenbaum Rubin, Jonathan's wife

- Chair of the Sisterhood of Congregation Ohr Chaim, Miami Beach, Florida, 1993-1994

- President of Sisterhood of Toras Emes Academy, 1992-95.

- Editor of "A Taste of TEAMwork Cookbook" published mid-1990s

Daniel Rubin - my son

- Served as an officer in the Israel Defense Forces, 1984-1987.

Rebecca Rubin Herman - my daughter

- Teacher, M'Ayanot Yeshiva High School for Girls, Teaneck New Jersey, 2012-2014

Pamela (Tzippora) Katz Moshe - Robert's daughter

- Teacher, Temple Israel Hebrew School, Natick, Massachusetts, 1984-85

- Teacher, Temple Shalom Emeth, Burlington, Massachusetts, 1986-87
- Teacher, Beth Rivka High School for Girls, Crown Heights, Brooklyn, New York, 1990-91
- Teacher, Mamlachti Dati, Ramot, Israel 1991
- Creator, Producer, Hostess of "Word City", a Jewish Children's TV Show, Manhattan Neighborhood Network, Public Access Television, Channel 34, 1995-96

Jeffrey Kurn - my nephew, Neal's son
- Member of the Jewish Community Relations Council of the Jewish Community Federation of South Peninsula, San Francisco Bay Area, California, 2005-06.

Lynn Fulton Kurn - Jeffrey's wife
- President of Congregation Beth Jacob, Redwood City, California, 2000-02.

Sharon Ilene Marcus-Kurn - Neal's daughter
- Chair of the Religious School Board and Board of Directors, Temple Emanuel, Kensington, Maryland

GENERATION SIX

Rebecca with her daughter Liora, 1995

Yehoshah Sova - Jonathan's son-in-law, Jessica's husband

- Teacher, Yeshiva Toras Chaim-Toras Emes, No. Miami Beach, Florida, 2014-Present

- Rav of Congregation Keter Sion, Miami Beach, Florida, 2014-present

Abigail Lerner Rubin - Raphael's and Rene's daughter-in-law, Jascha Rubin's Wife

- Assistant director of Volunteer Services, Jewish Association for Services for the Aged, New York City, 2008-2009

- Volunteer Services Manager, Jewish Board of Family and Children's Services, New York City, 2012-2013

- Program Director, Tikva: Advocates for the Jewish Mentally Ill, Philadelphia, Pennsylvania, 2014-2015

Nira Rubin Shain - Wife of Will Shain, Daughter of Daniel and Esther Rubin, Barbara's Granddaughter
- Teacher, New England Hebrew Academy, Brookline, Massachusetts, 2010s

Avrohom Moshe - Pamela's son, Robert's grandson
- Student body president, South Florida Jewish Academy, 2014-2015.

GENERATION SEVEN

Daniel Mordechai Rubin, 2015

What does the future hold? A harbinger …

Daniel Mordechai Rubin, son of Joshua and Dina Rubin, Grandson of Jonathan and Abby Rubin, Barbara's Great-grandson
- Valedictorian of four kindergarten classes of Yesode HaTorah, Toronto, Canada. Yiddish and Hebrew speaker extraordinaire, age 6, 2015.

Bibliography

1. *The Emersonian, 1928,* Emerson College Yearbook, Emerson College, Boston, Massachusetts. Photos and information for Jane Freeman Kurn.

2. *The University of Pennsylvania Yearbook, 1928*, the University of Pennsylvania, Philadelphia, Pennsylvania. Photos and information for Sam Kurnitsky/Kurn.

3. Michael Hoberman, *How Strange It Seems: The Cultural Life of Jews in Small Town New England.* University of Massachusetts Press, Amherst 2008. Photos of Rod's and Pyenson's.

4. Adeline Seamon Barowsky, *The Two of Us: Memories.* Marcus Printing, Holyoke, Massachusetts, 1985.